BLOOD LEGACY

Robert Franklin Godwin III

BLOOD LEGACY

Copyright 2024 – Robert Franklin Godwin III

Print Version ISBN – 978-1-949802-42-9

Published by Black Pawn Press

FIRST EDITION

Contents

The Container – Part One

Matthew 25:41 "Depart from me, cursed one, go to the Devil."

A deep-water port somewhere in the Black Sea

Ulysses stands close to the base of the gantry crane. Harder to see. Harder to be seen. The sun will be up soon. The sounds of the angry mob echo through the stacks of containers.

Where is that damn container? His mind races. *My whole life, centuries of memories, lost in the raid on my family's mansion. Only a few precious items remain after the looting. And one, just one, is what I need now.*

A long voyage is in front of him. Time to rest and gather strength. Bringing the only family he has back to where she can rest. His mother needs him now. The table has turned because it was Ulysses that had always needed her.

On the run since the sun last set, Ulysses knows the container, number FF6, was scheduled to load onto a freighter. It should be in the front row, but he would be exposed crossing to the open area under the gantry.

The noise from the mob grows louder. They are closing in. The crane operator sees a figure running toward the containers. He takes a quick nip from a whiskey flask and hides it deep in a shelf. Sliding the window open, the operator uses his binoculars to get a closer look and yells to the shadowy figure.

"Hey! Mister! It ain't safe to be under the crane!"

Ulysses looks up. "I'm looking for a container. FF6."

"You ain't supposed to be here. Besides, they've all been sealed by the Port Authority. You can't get in 'em."

Ulysses sees a necklace with a crucifix hanging from the operator's neck. It is polished silver, reflecting the many lights in the loading area. Wincing on each flash from the cross, he covers his eyes.

Ulysses yells up to the operator, "I am a priest. The family asked me to bless the container. I do not need to be inside."

"Oh, Father, I am sorry but…" the operator crosses himself, "Wait a minute. Let me check the manifest. What was the number again?"

"FF6," Ulysses yells back.

"Oh. It's too late. I loaded it an hour ago. It's on the *Merciful Sea*. She left the docks already. I'm sorry, Father."

Ulysses pleads, "How do I contact them?"

"How should I know?" The operator looks down from the booth. "Say, what kind of priest are you? Where are your vestments? You got any paperwork? How'd you even get on the docks?" Out of the misty darkness, a ship's horn blasts. "Well, I'll be damned. It's the *Merciful Sea*."

The operator leans out his window to call down to Ulysses. "Hey, that's the ship!" He scans the dock but Ulysses isn't there. "Huh, where'd he go?"

Turning around, he sees Ulysses standing in front of the booth's control dashboard. "How the hell did you get in here?"

Ulysses peers into the operator's eyes and with a lightning quick move of his hand, the operator is frozen stiff. As his eyes widen, he slowly slips back into his seat. A small drop of blood falls on his hand. The operator's eyes roll upward in his head as he collapses into the chair.

Ulysses grimaces and spits on the floor. "Too much Palinka, my friend. It will kill you, and it ruins the palate experience. Stay calm. You will be fine." He takes a tissue from the box on the dashboard and wipes away the small drop of blood from the corner of his mouth.

The operator comes to a few minutes later. He looks up and sees Ulysses outside the booth, his cape flowing in the harbor wind.

Still groggy, the operator calls out, "Get back in here! That's an eighty foot fall!" He gasps as he sees Ulysses leap into the air and fly out over the water, landing on the *Merciful Sea*. The operator's eyes roll up again as he faints, falling back into his chair.

Several moments pass. Banging on the window, the leader of the mob tries to stir the operator. Dizzy and weak, the operator regains consciousness and reaching over, unlatches the door.

The mob leader speaks. "We have a warrant for an escaped criminal for assaulting a few dozen people. You seen anyone on these docks since yesterday around sunset?"

Stunned and weak, the operator looks up and says, "He flew over the harbor." Gasping for air, he collapses onto the dashboard, hitting the crane controls. The booth shakes violently. The flask of Palinka falls from the shelf where it was hidden.

The leader reaches down, opens the flask and sniffs. "Oh great, heavy crane operator drunk on the job. Look at you, pale white. Like every drop of blood has drained from your body. We're reporting you to the Harbor Master."

The operator just moans.

Disgusted, the leader looks out over the waters. "He flew over the water. Drunken fool. Shit."

He hurls the flask through the open window into the harbor.

The ship's horn blows a warning, leaving on the morning tides to the open sea.

Ulysses stands atop a container stacked on the deck of the *Merciful Sea*. The ocean breeze gently furls his cape. He leaps down and rests his hand on the container label, FF6. With a slight push, he opens a hidden side door.

The distant horizon glows with a golden aura as the sun is about to rise. As Ulysses steps inside, he stops and takes one last look outside. Wondering what her voice was like, he whispers words – a lullaby his mother was denied singing to soothe him.

Little one, who dwelt in this house of darkness. Well, you are outside now. You have seen the light of the sun.

Ulysses closes the door. It seals without a visible trace.

Ulysses at the Gates of Jerusalem

Matthew 27:46 "My God. My God, why have you forsaken me?"

Late Spring, 43 A.D.

In a small hovel by the Damascus Gate in old Jerusalem, Filius Caligula sits with his young son. Roman soldiers overwhelm the city. Marching out of the gate at sunrise, they throw stale bread to the poor. A boy scrambles for the food scraps and brings them to his elderly father.

Filius watches his motherless son brushing the gravel and dirt from the bread.

"Son, be grateful for the food the soldiers cast off."

He looks to the sky and back at his son. "Come inside. I must tell you this story. It is time for you to know why you had no mother to nurture you from her breast, to soothe you with lullabies, to teach you how to be a man, and to learn how the world challenges you. Her brother committed sins and was rewarded with worthless worldly treasure. Judas testified to the secrets held by the King of the Jews."

Filius' hands wave and create shadows from the small fireplace's warm light as his son watches with wide eyes.

"Yes, Jesus of Nazareth told his disciples he was the King, and this was to be kept from all of his followers. Judas took the silver pieces and when he betrayed the confidence placed in him by the Son of God, his guilt overwhelmed him. At the place of the skull, at Golgotha, he was horrified by the gruesome gore of Jesus's torment. He touched the cross and buried his face in his blood-covered hands as he cried and howled his grief, screaming to God to forgive him for his treachery."

Filius continues, "Leaving the silver pieces in a pool of blood, he found his way home and there, still seeking forgiveness, hung himself. As he slowly suffocated, the last words he heard were spoken by a voice from the heavens."

A godly grief produces a repentance that leads to salvation without regret. Your worldly grief produces only death. You shall be neither in Heaven nor in Hell, but remain in earthly turmoil.

"His body hung until your mother, against the will of the village, cut him down. The Sanhedrin accused your mother of heresy, a seditious act, my young wife bearing you, my son, and instructed the Mequbbal mystic to curse her soul."

She shall live forever, and only find sustenance in the blood of living beings. No death can bring her salvation and the curse on Judas's head is now upon her, and her children that she will bear, and their children, and so it shall be.

Filius watches a mask of confusion and sadness come over his son's face. He continues the story.

"But the villagers were not satisfied with the curse. The moment she gave birth, she was dragged to Calvary. A stake was driven through her young heart, nailing her to the wooden cross of Jesus. Half alive, she violently thrashed, screaming for mercy, until her pleas shortened to gasps, until she drew a shallow breath for the last time. The village elder ripped our newborn boy from my arms. He used a holy dagger to carve two marks into the nape of the baby's neck."

"The elder announced to the crowd, 'Let these two scars warn every soul of the danger of this curse!'"

The tired and sorrowful father looks at his son, whose tears stream down his young, dirty face.

"And you, my son, bear that curse. Bread offers a meal, but blood is life. And you must seek it, as you shall never die, never know repentance, and never be forgiven."

The son, Ulysses, bore countless children, and turned many mortals into eternal disciples, chased from village to village, saddened by their fate, cursed to live without redemption, in a limbo only vampires can know.

Madison and Orphan

Genesis 22:2 "Take your son, your only son, whom you love, and sacrifice him."

Renville County, Minnesota, early 21st century.

In a remote edge of Olaf Bathory's farm, he and Doc Willard, the Renville County large animal veterinarian, stands over a calving cow. The animal is in great distress. This has been going on for more than six hours, longer than normal for a cow that has calved many times.

Doc Willard reaches into the cow and grasps the calf's head. Pulling gently, the head emerges but the calf does not drop. Her final heave, with the help of Olaf, the calf's hooves appear and she falls free. The small calf is undersized and crying for her mother. The mother cow drops to her knees, moaning mournfully.

Doc Willard looks over to Olaf and says that the mother will need to be put down. "It's best she is butchered for the meat you can get. She will not recover."

Looking at Olaf, he continues, "That cow should not have been bred. She's too old. You know that, Olaf." He looks to the newborn and back at Olaf. "This calf will not make it."

Olaf, unrepentant, slowly says, "Madison will have to nurse the calf. She has the touch."

Doc looks at Olaf. "I am tagging her now." He takes out his tag applicator to attach the button. "I'm registering the death of the mother with the county, so take care of her today. As for the calf, if she reaches maturity, I will have a claim to pay my bill. I know it's been rough, Olaf. Rough enough for everyone these past two years. But your carelessness… well, I can't afford to support bad farming."

Olaf stands silent, then turns to the vet. "Do what you need to, Doc."

Madison and her young sisters are waiting at the gate. She wonders what the girls think about this. They haven't seen a cow calve before. Madison watched both of her sisters birthed.

Olaf turns and hollers for Madison to come. She tells the girls to stay put and runs up to her father and kneels to pet the mother cow.

Olaf says without emotion, "Get the bolt-gun and the CO2 tank. Bring the utility tractor. She can't make it back to the slaughter slab for processing."

Madison asks, "What about the baby?"

"She's now your responsibility, and we need her to make it."

"You will need to hand feed her for the next four months." Doc Willard adds. "She can't process cud right now, maybe never."

Madison pets the calf and dries her with a large rag. Olaf waves for her to do something. "Go on, git!"

Madison carries the newborn to the gate. Her sisters are curious and excited. "What are you going to name her?"

"Orphan," Madison replies with a little smile. The calf looks up and bleats.

Olaf becomes impatient and yells, "Madison, now!"

Madison returns driving the utility tractor, as she has done since she was seven-years-old. Olaf takes the bolt gun and attaches it to the CO2 tank. He bleeds the line of air, testing the gun.

"Go join your sisters," Olaf says coldly.

Madison ignores him and pets the mother cow.

Doc Willard looks at her. "Come with me, child."

Getting to the gate with the newborn calf, Doc Willard instructs Madison. "Feed her colostrum. Get it from the dams in your herd. First feeding must be in the next few hours, then twelve hours later. Every twelve hours for two weeks. No more, no less."

He looks at his pocket watch, then places it back in his vest.

He takes a moment and looks at Madison and her sisters. They are fussing over the calf. He says in a somber tone, "It's not a pet." With that, Doc Willard walks off.

In the distance, Madison watches her father lean over the mother, watches the cow's body jerk, and then hears the delayed pop of the bolt-gun. She instinctively covers the eyes of the calf.

State Fair 4H Competition

Job 4:13-16 "...disquieting thoughts from the visions of the night."

Falcon Heights, Minnesota. August.

The Minnesota Junior Farmer arena is filled with noisy fans. Over the loudspeaker the announcer barks out, "And now for the winning heifer in this year's State Fair, ORPHAN, raised by Madison Bathory!" The crowd cheers.

Now fourteen, Madison accepts the trophy, waves to the cheering crowd, and comes over to the stands to show her father and Doc Willard. Expressionless, Olaf looks over the trophy. Handing her a ten-dollar bill, he instructs Madison to take her sisters for cotton candy and ice cream.

The competition judge walks over and hands Olaf the $1,000 prize money.

Doc Willard looks at the cash. "Olaf..."

Olaf interrupts. "I know Doc, I know." He peels off several bills, turns to face Doc Willard and handing him the money says, "The debt it paid."

Doc looks Olaf in the eyes. "I wasn't going to ask for the money. You have something more important than cash. It was the care Madison gave. She has the gift. Almost magical, saving the calf. You raised a real farmer."

Olaf, stone-faced, looks at Doc. "You set the terms. I paid the debt. That is farming, too. Good farming."

The girls spent the ten dollars on deep-fried Twinkies. Madison's trophy is filled sky-high with ice cream, dripping down the sides from the summer heat. The lights on the Ferris wheel and carousel make Madison's head spin. She is in a dreamlike state. Her sisters are bragging about her to every person they pass. She feels like she's floating just above the ground, elevated to a status, a sense of purpose, glowing with pride.

The trio returns to the arena. A small crowd is watching the exsanguinating demonstration. The sisters shout in unison, "Maddy! Look!"

Madison screams in horror. She sees Orphan hanging by a single hoof from the rafters, being drained. Tears streaming down, she runs to the stage, slipping on the pool of blood growing under Orphan.

Covered in red from head to toe, Madison looks up at her father. He is showered with the blood coming from Orphan. Olaf speaks in a thundering echoed voice. "I am a good farmer!" Looking down at Madison he commands, "Bring me the bolt-gun."

Madison looks at him in horror. "No!"

He smiles. It's the first smile she's seen of his since her mother died. His teeth are bright, and a glow appears around his head. Olaf raises the bolt-gun to his temple and pulls the trigger.

The 'pop' sounds, and Madison jerks awake. This is the third night in a row for this nightmare. Her head is on the pillow, she is breathing hard, and sweating. She throws off the cover and sits on the edge of the bed. Her cellmate looks down from the top bunk and whispers, "You keep waking me up and your ass is getting kicked, ¿Entiendes perra?"

Madison grunts, reaches under her mattress and fumbles for the stash of cigarettes. These are her brand, Gitanes. The French girl in Cell Block D has them. $5.00 each, in for being a mule. Black heroin. Innocent, she claims. Nobody with black heroin is innocent. She'll be here a while.

Madison strikes a match with her thumbnail. No lighters are allowed. The cellmate, still watching her warns, "You better blow the smoke down el trono."

Madison fills the end of the cigarette with kief.

"The guards patrol in ten minutes. Get us caught and I cut you. In the face! ¿Lo entiendes, cono?"

Ignoring the threat, Madison takes a deep hit and muffles her cough. Bending over the toilet, she blows the smoke coordinated with a flush. She uses her pillow to wipe the mist from her face. Laying back down, one last cough in the crook of her arm, Madison slowly falls back to sleep.

Nick Charles, Special Agent

Genesis 1:26 "And God said, 'Let us make man in our own image.'"

The Everglades, present day

The agency-issued sedan was no match for the muddy road leading to the research facility. Passing businesses on the edge of the swamp, they are slowly being swallowed by the rising waters.

"Turn right at the sign for the container storage yard," the report read. The GPS announces, "There is another 4.3 miles of unmaintained frontage road to get to your destination." The road to the institute is bordered on both sides by the rising swamp. Spanish moss hangs low on the trees catching the side mirrors and wipers.

ICE Agent Nick Charles' regulation boots won't be enough to stay dry, much less stay clean in these sunken parts of the swamps. He turns and glances to see if the waders are in the back seat. Too many times Nick has had to pull the bodies of desperate immigrants from the swampy sludge, half-eaten by gators and crabs, picked at by red and black vultures.

Arriving at the entrance to the Human Alternative Lifeforms Institute, the car is of no further use. The gated entrance is at least a foot under water. A rickety wooden walkway leads to the front service building. The institute has been condemned since the rising waters submerged the first floors of the two main buildings and the library is being cleared before it sinks any further.

Josiah Jakes, groundskeeper, sits in a rocking chair on the porch of the wooden shack serving as his office. He has a simple hand fan slowly waving the air around his face. His other hand, fingers spread wide, hold open the pages of a bible on his lap.

Nick approaches and introduces himself. "I am ICE Agent Charles." He shows his badge. "Are you Josiah Jakes?"

Josiah looks down to Nick standing on the boardwalk. "Yes, sir. JJ most call me. You here 'cause the Pr'fessor called about the intruder?"

Nick puts the badge back on his service belt. His hand rests on the handle of the holstered automatic firearm. "I need to ask you some questions, Mr. Jakes."

"JJ, most call me. No point in that, Mr. Charles."

Nick corrects him quickly. "Agent Charles."

"I don't know nuthin' 'bout it. Pr'fessor Skogman is who you need to talk to."

Taking notes in a small spiral-bound pad, Nick asks "The first name?"

JJ's eyes roll up in his head. "I don't rightly know. Just Pr'fessor." He swats at a mosquito with the fan.

"Building 2, third floor. First floor is two feet under water."

JJ looks down at the bible in his lap. "Loaned it to me, this bible, so I could read a verse to the workers. To calm them after seeing the intruder."

Nick looks up at JJ. "And? Do you have a description?"

JJ ignores the query and begins reading. "Leviticus 17:11. Never liked the bible. On Sundays, Pastor Jones used to hit us in the back of the head saying 'Everything about everybody and every living thing is in this book. Includin' everything about you, boy!'" JJ chuckles.

Nick is growing impatient. "What does that have to do with the Professor?"

JJ slowly answers, "Oh nuthin' I suppose. Just said read the verse."

"And?"

JJ reads, "The life of the flesh is in the blood. Now what you s'ppose that means? I mean about that intruder?"

Nick, shaking his head turns back to go to the car. "I'm getting my waders from the car."

JJ shouts after, "Bring a lantern. Or use mine. Gets dark early this time of year. First floor got no lights. Take this bible back to the Professor, sir, please."

As Nick heads towards Building 2, he watches JJ board a Jon boat. Over the hum of the outboard motor, JJ calls, "Don't forget that bible. It's an old one. Keep it dry."

"I'm headed home." JJ announces. "Faster by boat. The access road is flooded. It ain't comin' back. Takes me 20 minutes by boat. An hour to get to the highway by car. Yes sir, the boat. You got about hour of decent light left. Full moon might help if it don't cloud up." And with that, JJ twists the throttle and speeds off into the mangroves.

Nick walks up to Building 2. Putting on the waders he struggles to push open the front doors tangled with vines. Moving slowly through waist-high water, Nick hears the flutter of dozens of wings overhead. Something swims by. A rat, maybe.

Clambering up the staircase he makes it to the third floor's cavernous room. At the distant end, a tall ornate window silhouettes a person hunched over a large open book.

"Professor Skawagmon?" he shouts.

A deep gravelly voice responds, "It's Skogman. Long 'o', the 'g' is silent."

Nick notes the comment in his pad "You put a call into the ICE office about an incident, a possible illegal immigrant sighting."

"Close, but not quite. I told them a lifeform that looked human." She takes a long drag from the half-smoked cigarette and extinguishes it in an overflowing ashtray.

Nick, removing the waders, stops and looks up. "Lifeform?" he asks suspiciously.

"Yes, and you are?"

"Agent Charles."

"Agent Charles. I hoped they'd send you. And yes, lifeform."

"Go on."

Professor Grethe Skogman removes her glasses from the bridge of her nose and lets them hang from the lanyard around her neck. Leaning back, she picks up an ornate silver cigarette case from her desk. Grethe gestures with the case, offering a smoke "They're French." Nick waves it off. Lighting the fresh unfiltered cigarette, she continues her tale.

"The workers shoring up the first floor saw him."

"Him?" Nick questions.

"By their description of a cape, bouffant hairdo, yes, a *him*."

"When exactly was this sighting?"

"Last Friday at sunset, just as the workers were finishing for the day. But please, let me finish without interruption."

Nick waves his hand, surrenders the moment.

"The lighting made it difficult for them to see. The ground fog always comes up this time of year and the setting sun turns everything into a silhouette."

Grethe pauses.

Frustrated, Nick checks the report and reads, "Was floating above the water. Then disappeared into the mangroves." He snaps the pad shut. "Floating. In a boat? A raft? A skiff? Listen Professor, did you witness any this? Or is it all hearsay from the day workers? They're Haitian, right? Given to voodoo and zombies?"

"Your prejudice aside, Agent Charles, all eight of them saw this *incident* as you call it. They all, to a one, said he was 15 feet above the water surface."

"With all due respect, setting aside my prejudice, what a crock."

"I know your background, Agent Charles. I checked you out with my contacts at Airborne Object Institute. You believe there are alien beings."

"I investigated reports. As for belief, to a one, all were more believable than this. One sighting? Please."

Grethe scoffs, "I guess we are done here."

"Not yet. And I am in a different business now. Illegals. I'm not swallowing your worker's stories. But there has been activity suggesting something's afoot."

Grethe leans forward.

Nick continues, "A ship arrived last month. The *Merciful Sea*. Several crew members had mysterious ailments. All involved a heavy loss of blood. Part of our mission is to prevent diseases entering the States. Immigrants, illegal ones, are central to this threat."

Grethe makes busy with the papers on her desk, disengaging from Nick.

He raises his voice. "There is a group of climate activists. They have been secretly recruiting militant activists, including mercenaries, from other countries. Brazil, Columbia, Malaysia, eastern Europe, anywhere there are climate activists, anywhere there are military contractors. We captured three crossing in Minnesota from Canada. They all had criminal records from militaristic violence against oil, coal and other corporate energy companies."

Grethe, getting impatient, has had enough of the lecture "I only reported what I was told. I am not involved in climate protests. Only the effect climate has on genetic structure. And the topic is likely beyond your ken."

Nick ignores the condescension.

"Specifically, we are looking for members of CAN. They have been increasing their threats and may be behind getting these climate commandos across the border. The leader is a certain Madison Bathory. She was released from a Canadian facility four months ago. We intercepted text communication between south Florida and the container ship. We think it's her, the ringleader." The professor is attentive. And suspicious. 'What does that have to do with me?"

"We think she is in the everglades. Other than that, it probably has nothing to do with you, or this institute."

"Then I do think we are done here." Grethe gestures to the stairwell. "Do you need me to show you the way out?"

"If *him* floats by again, give me call." Nick flips his card onto Grethe's desk.

Grethe responds "Humph." Replaces her glasses, and resumes reading the volume on her desk.

Nick turns to leave. Something scurries at his feet. Nick figures a rat. Or snake. They tend to go together.

Professor Grethe Skogman

Proverbs 14:1 "The wise woman builds her house, But the foolish one pulls it down."

Professor Grethe Skogman is the last of the founding administrators of the Human Alternative Lifeforms Institute (HALI). The old mansion housing the institute has been slowly undermined by the rising waters on the southern edges of the Florida Everglades.

Grethe hates the humid climate and profusion of mosquitos, flying cockroaches and black flies. It is her devotion to the recently defunded programs she was elemental in designing that kept her here these past few years, despite the humiliations she endured.

She labors daily over the numerous articles and scholarly papers that document the ample evidence of alternate life forms. Grethe realizes she can claim ownership over this research due to the final decision to close the institute. The result declassified all remaining documents. She could now publish freely, and she intends to do so.

"The world needs to know that multiple human variants exist." she wrote in the JOURNAL OF GENETIC MUTATION DISORDERS. Grethe's colleagues dismissed the validity of the findings and signed an open letter to the journal to protest publishing Professor Skogman on any topic.

Grethe is younger than her recently retired colleagues. She had been the wunderkind entering Cambridge at 16 and receiving a Harvard doctorate by age 21.

Her genomic research of mutant genes in human DNA won numerous grants and the initial funding that made the HALI facility possible. But one by one, colleagues grew weary of her eccentric behavior and obsession with outlandish theories on abnormal human lifeforms.

After the discovery of tampering with bodies recovered from unusual and unexplained accidents, the Board of Governors stripped Grethe of professor status, demoting her to Research Archivist.

Humiliated, Grethe secretly gathered the documents and collected specimens, the physical evidence in jars filled with formaldehyde, vials of blood samples, now lining every shelf in the vast library. With the closing of HALI formally announced, it is all hers.

When she learned from Agent Charles that one of the climate activists was a certain Madison Bathory, identified as leader of the climate activists, Grethe immediately recognized the name. Years ago, Madison violently disrupted a conference where the Professor was keynote speaker. Called as a witness at her trial, Grethe was surprised Madison had chosen to act as her own attorney. She was captivated by the activist's passion and display of emotional intelligence. Madison was not some neophyte acting out for attention.

Insulting the judge, the prosecutor, and the court staff, she created a forum in the courtroom where the issues of climate change affecting humans took center stage.

Claiming climate change would wipe out humans within two decades drew derisive laughter from prosecution. Enraged, Madison physically attacked her opponent.

The incident gained her international notoriety. She also garnered a 13-month sentence in a federal detention center.

The Container - Part 2

Isaiah 30:20 "And your ears shall hear a word behind you, saying: This is the way, walk in it."

Wearing a colorful pleated skirt, a patterned blouse, and long apron, the old woman eyes the group of three coming through the front gate of Clementina's Container Corral.

Madison, Hannah, and Nolan walk toward the office porch. A tattered rope stretches between pillars supporting a decaying roof. Clothing draped over it to dry. A ragged Romanian football flag covers the windows. Strands of plaited garlic hang across the entire length of the porch.

The visitors, all in their twenties, look at each other and giggle. Nolan whispers, "She looks like a Gypsy." Hannah corrects him, "Romani. They're Romani. Gypsy is like using the 'N' word."

Madison looks over to the woman sitting on a sagging couch and says, "We're here to pick up furniture from the auction."

The woman fans herself with a folded Racing Form. She finally speaks with a heavy eastern European accent, "You have receipt with container number?"

Madison pulls the receipt from her jeans pocket and holds it out. The old lady snarls, "Do you expect me to get up?"

Leaning on railing, Madison asks, "Are you Clementina?"

"Clementina is dead, many years. You want me to raise her from the tomb?"

Hannah intercedes, "We just want to get our furniture." She grabs the receipt from Madison and walks up the stairs to the woman. Hannah asks "Do you make sure the containers are sprayed for spiders and ants? And what about rats?"

The woman stares down Hannah, "The swamp crabs take care of the rats. Spiders are your problem." Nolan speaks up. "We can spray for the spiders and ants. Let's get going."

"Container FF6." The woman stops reading and slowly looks up at Madison. Her stern countenance conveyed her reticence. "Vano!" she shouts, still staring at Madison. A man with a long gray beard and many facial piercings, cracks open the ragged screen door. The woman gestures toward Madison and her friends and in a lowered voice says, "Have Timbo take them to Area E1, container FF6."

A young boy, no more than ten years old, opens the creaking screen door. Without word, he gestures to Madison and the others to follow him. A small unkempt mutt scurries out on the Timbo's heels. Nolan reaches over to pet the animal but is met with a low growl. Limping slightly, the dog circles the group as they make their way. The area alongside the path is muddy. Stacks of containers sink into the ground. At the end of the storage canyons, a rusty container stands alone. Once again, the boy gestures, this time towards the container. He moves no further. The dog whimpers, staying close to Timbo.

Nolan breaks the awkward silence, looking at the stack of containers with water halfway around them. "Good thing ours is on high ground. Those will be under water after the rains." Hannah shrugs, "I guess..."

The group approaches the container. As they walk, a dark cloud covers the sun, and a shadowless world takes hold.
Nolan shouts back to Timbo, "How do we open this thing? The latch is welded over."

Timbo points over to a rickety metal tool shed. Nolan struggles with the misshapen door. He pulls one more time and it partially opens.

"Ouch!" Nolan looks at his hand, "I found a sledgehammer and chisel. I cut my hand." The blood drips onto the hammer. Nolan pulls out the red bandana he wears to keep the hair out of his eyes.

Standing between Timbo and Hannah, the dog barks furiously. It tugs at Timbo's pants and to pull him away. Timbo's eyes get big when he sees the blood and runs way, looking back, calling for the dog to follow.

Nolan wraps his bandana over the wound, "Wow, sure is bleeding a lot for a small scratch."

Madison says, "I am sure you'll live. You have plenty of blood, a little scratch isn't going to kill you. But just in case, get this open now." They all giggle.

The three of them gather around the lock. Madison holds the chisel. Hannah grips the door handle. "Don't miss!" Madison warns Nolan. He raises the hammer, misses the chisel, slams it down on the latch.

The welded latch breaks apart. Metal fragments all over the group. Each of them has small scratches. Every scratch oozes blood.

Nolan exclaims, "We are the walking wounded."

"Shit." Hannah watches the slow bleed from her wound.

Madison says in a low voice, "Wait. Quiet. I heard something inside."

Mysterious Traveler

Exodus 22:21 "Thou shalt not vex a stranger or oppress him."

The clouds have now completely covered the sun. A ground fog slowly creeps up from the swamp waters. The sinking containers are engulfed and appear to float on an undulating grey field. A large sheet of plywood on the side of the container moves revealing a face in the shadows. A heavily accented voice asks, "What do you want?"

Nolan whispers, "There was an opening this whole time!" Hannah shrieks "Who are you?" Madison confronts the mysterious person "What are you doing in our container?"

A man pushes the plywood aside. He is groomed and well dressed and appears to be in his late thirties. Madison, Nolan, and Hannah, standing shoulder to shoulder grip the tools they used on the lock.

"There is no need to be fearful, I mean no harm." The man gestures toward the side opening. "Please. Go in and you will find your furniture is in good condition."

The three looked at each other. Madison turns and says, "Okay, okay. I will check it out. You guys stay here. Where's the flashlight?" "You," gesturing to the stranger, "stay out here until I'm done."

He responds, "If you prefer." Nolan, under his breath "What is this guy, a butler?"

Madison steps into the container. She turns on the flashlight. It flickers. Madison shakes it, and light is back on. All the furniture is wrapped except one piece. She approaches. She runs the beam along the length. "What the hell?"

Madison storms out of the container. "What the hell is a coffin doing in there?"

The stranger answers calmly "There was nothing else that was suitable for sleeping."

The three say in semi-unison, "Who the hell are you?" "What is your name?" "How did you get here?"

"My name is Ulysses. I come from the Black Sea, a port on the Danube. It was a long voyage."

Madison, suspicious, "There aren't any accommodations in there. No water, no bathroom, no lights..."

"Please you will find that I have perfect hygiene, and nothing is damaged, or spoiled. What I do ask is if you can provide a suitable space for me to reside. I can pay a fair price. I can also help you set up your new accommodations."

Madison replies, "The furniture is for an office. Our headquarters. It is not an apartment."

Hannah whispers to Madison, "We can use the money. And he can provide security at night. The building is abandoned and there is plenty of space."

Nolan chimes in, "I agree with Hannah. We need the money. Besides, I do most of my work late at night. Would be nice to have another body around."

Madison pauses for a moment.

"Mr. Ulysses. We can use your help. There are a few things you need to know about us. We are activists. Climate change and the threat to human survival is our cause, our raison d'être."

Ulysses listens to the excitement in the young people's voices. Their energy and vitality are stirring emotions. Ulysses understands saving humanity is also his means to survival. "Blood is life" his father taught him.

Hannah interjects, "But we don't get violent. No bombs or kidnappings. We take advantage of big events."

Nolan adds, "Yeah. Sporting events, concerts. Wherever there are lots of people and cameras. We don't spin a sign on a street corner."

Madison continues, "And, well, essentially we are making people aware that they can only save themselves from themselves. It can get rough. People in this country hate change."

Ulysses is fascinated with their sophisms, their crude actions; it is fate thinly disguised.

Madison adds, "You need to know this before you work with us. One other thing. We are secret, underground is where we thrive. Not literally. But we stay off the grid as much as possible."

Ulysses assures the group "I have been discrete my entire life. I understand the need for secrecy is essential."

Nolan leans in, "Yeah. Under the radar. We are stealthy."

Ulysses looks into the eyes of each of them, "I embrace your mission and its importance. Please let me join you."

Madison says, "Well, what we have is one well-dressed security guard." Looking Ulysses up and down "What do you do? What is your skill?"

"I am a people person and can be very persuasive. I will people over. Perhaps this is a useful skill for you?"

Madison corrects him, "You mean 'win' people over."

Ulysses concedes, "As you wish, ah yes, win them over."

"Hmmm..." Madison locks on Ulysses' eyes, and suppresses her natural suspicion, "Perhaps it is. Useful that is."

With a sanguine look Ulysses says, "And please, call me Uly."

All three respond "Hey Uly!"

Madison adds, "Useful Uly it is. Welcome aboard."

Uly now has two missions on this voyage to America. He will join the team and help them bring awareness to humans. Uly is struck by the irony of saving the people he must harvest to survive, the same people who condemned his mother and laid the curse upon his head.

The blood legacy must continue and clearing his mother from the wrongful charge of heresy that rules his everyday life, from sunset to sunrise.

Uly reaches out and grips each hand, European style. The team closes with high fives, American style.

The Facility

Job 19:13-14 "…my friends have turned against me."

Three Years Earlier

Professor Skogman arrives at the entrance to the state facility for women. She has decided this attempt to visit Madison, the fourth, will be the last.

The gate guard greets her, "Well, Professor, it looks like the fourth time is the charm. Inmate Bathory has accepted your request for a visit." The Professor smiles. At last, she will have a discussion with a force, a person who makes an impact simply by being who they are.

The large metal door opens with the hum of an electric motor. It inches across the threshold, creaking to a stop. The gate guard motions her to move forward to the glass window.

The entry clerk does not look up.

"Please state your name."

"Professor Skogman."

"Your first name is professor?"

"Uh, no Grethe. Grethe Skogman."

"Spell it."

"Look, I've been here several times…"

"Spell it or be denied entrance."

"Grethe. G-r-e-t-h-e, Skogman S-k-o-g-m-a-n"

"Do you have any food items, sharp objects or weapon of any kind?"

"Of course not! No weapons!"

The guard looks up, stares for a moment.

"When the green light flashes, enter."

The barred door to the visitor rooms opens with metallic creaks. Grethe steps forward and continues down a hallway brightly lit with buzzing fluorescent tubes. Reaching the end of the hallway a guard scans her with a metal detector.

"This seems like a lot of procedure for a minimum-security prison."

The visitation guard corrects her. "Facility, Professor. Not a prison."

"Of course."

"Proceed to your left. The meeting area is the third door. Inmate Bathory will join you."

Grethe walks down the hall to the third door. It is reinforced with steel bars and a narrow wire-mesh security window. A voice on the loudspeaker instructs her to sit at booth number two.

Thick plexiglass separates her from the other side where an empty chair waits for Madison. A small box of alcohol wipes sits next to the phone. Grethe lifts the handset and starts to untwist the knotted cord. Two wipes are hardly enough to clean the phone.

She is startled by a robotic voice, "Inmate is entering."

Madison sits, facing the professor. The guard behind her leans into the booth from the doorjamb. The guard looks over Grethe and says something to Madison. There is no sound.

The voice on the loudspeaker instructs Grethe to pick up the phone.

She hesitates, shocked by the haggard look of Madison. It is not the vibrant young lady who commanded an international audience in the courtroom.

Grethe picks up the phone. "Hello Miss Bathory. I'm…"

Madison interrupts. "I know who you are. I saw you at the trial. What the fuck do you want from me?"

The professor does not flinch. "Your passion and commitment will do."

They stared at each other for a long moment. Madison cracks the slightest of smiles. "I'm listening."

Grethe re-focuses and starts explaining her interest to Madison. "My work, my life's work, is to make the world aware of what climate change, pollution-intensified climate change is doing to people. The impact of genetic mutations."

Madison holds up her hand. "I am concerned about genetic mutants in food sources: wheat, potatoes, cattle, fish."

Grethe raises her voice. "Not natural mutation, imposed disfiguring of the code. The amino acids are being polluted. They cannot be reliably controlled by the codons. Evidence of this is readily available but no one wants to listen."

Madison responds, raising her voice. "I want to put an end to pumping CO_2 into the atmosphere killing the ozone layer. Your institute? You deal with mutant people. Freaks of nature. That's just weird."

Grethe starts to protest that characterization.

Madison bursts out, "I'm done. Done with you trying to use me. You testified against me. You put me here. You say we have the same goals, and you betray me? And now you want my help? Piss off, you Judas."

She slams the phone onto the hook cutting her hand. Madison glares at Gerthe, then yells, "God damn it."

Madison wheels around, bangs on the secure door pleading, "Guard! Let me out of here!" Blood streaks the window as the guard opens the door.

Grethe sits stunned. She does not have a response. The feeling of rejection is the same after her colleagues wrote her off. Why can't Madison realize the importance of the mutations? How can she reject the threat to humans? To her mission?

She is startled when the guard comes up behind her, "The visit is over, Professor. Time to go." Grethe, looks up at the guard, slowly rises out of the chair and walks down the hallway to the exit.

Renfield Hess, CEO

Proverbs 29:2 "But when the wicked beareth rule, the people mourn."

Somewhere in Downtown Manhattan

The Coal Alliance (CA) CEO, Renfield Hess, arrives at the 50-story office complex precisely at 8:45 a.m., as he does for every monthly board meeting. He takes a moment and stares down the street vendor working at the elegant entrance.

"I've told you before, find a corner on some other street or I'll have vendor enforcement seize your cart."

Hess grabs the vendor by the collar. "The stench of the meat you cook, it pollutes the air. I can smell it on the 50th floor." Hess releases his grip on the vendor, grabs the framed license hanging on the side and tosses it to the curb.

The immigrant vendor cowers in the fear his license could be taken so easily. He runs to retrieve it. Hess spits on the grill where it boils away into steam and pushes through the glass doors.

At the security gate he confronts the doorman. "If you see him here again get rid of him. If I see him again I'm getting rid of you."

Hess throws his briefcase on the conveyor and passes through the scanner.

Outside, Ali, a regular customer, stops by the food cart. "Niki, Niki, Niki."

Without looking up, Niki greets Ali, "As-Salsam."
Ali says, "Gimme four gyros, cut'em in half. I'm buying for the office. Hey what happened to your license? It's all busted up!"

Niki, still looking down, "It's okay. No problem."

"Dude, your hand is bleeding. Get it bandaged before some jerk complains to the health department."

Niki shakes his head, eyes tearing, wipes down the grill, "Four gyros, cut in half. Coming right up!"

On the 50th floor the executive elevator doors open. Hess heads straight into the office bypassing reception and the C-suite. At the end of the main aisle. He sees the company's board members already seated at the conference table.

As Hess heads down the aisle exits the break room, Noah, the office gofer, rushes out of the break room, almost colliding with Hess. Stopping short and balancing a large donut box, he nervously greets the boss. "H-hello, sir. Good morning."
Hess responds, "Do you mind getting out of my way."

"Sorry, sir. I'm just giving out donuts. W-w-would you like one?"

"Donuts?" Hess asks with voice raised, "You're giving out donuts."

"Yes." Noah responds with a nervous smile. "The staff gets donuts on Thursdays."

By this time the office has taken notice of Hess's exchange with Noah. The cube farm workers slowly sink back into their chairs, out of sight. Helen, the Office Manager hovers nearby, staying several steps away, saying nothing.

Hess continues, "What's your name?"

"Noah, sir."

"Feeding the animals on the ark, Noah?"

Noah stammers, "Uh well, no, just Thursday donuts. They're a gift."

"That's a big box. How many donuts are there?"

"Uh, 18. I always get the dozen and a half deal."

"Which one did you get me?"

"I didn't know...I didn't get one for you."

"Which one should I have?"

Most of the office staff are peering over the top of their cubicle walls.

"Uh, people like the French cruller. I always get extra of those."

"The FRENCH Cruller?" Hess raises his voice.

"French? Hess is a German name. My father worked in the coal mines of Ruhr. And you offer me a French donut? I want a Bavarian Cream donut. Yes. I'll have a Bavarian Cream."

Noah can only stare.

Hess pushes harder, "Well? Where is my Bavarian Cream?"

"I-I-I didn't get any."

"No Bavarian Cream?" Hess looks around the office. Everyone watching the confrontation suddenly attacks their keyboards. Helen looks down.

"Well, here's what we're going to do. What *you* are going to do."

"Yes, sir?"

"Where is your desk?"

"It's-it's right here."

"All right. Put the box on your desk. Move your keyboard. Put the box right there. That's it." Hess motions for Helen to come over, "Helen, take a picture of this desk with the donuts. Right there."

The office workers are again looking to see what Hess is up to.

Hess leans close to Noah. "I am here until eight tonight. If I see one change to these donuts, one missing, one bite, you are out of a job."

Hess pulls pack from Noah's face. He scans the office as the workers turn away and hurriedly walk to their workstations.

Helen flips her hand, gesturing for Noah to sit. She says to Hess, "Sir, the board members are all here. Is there anything you need?"

Hess turns to Helen, "Donuts. Think about it. Is it worth your job too?"

In an acidulous tone, he announces through clenched teeth, "Good morning, everyone. Let's make it a productive day." Hess turns and continues to the board room.

Ali, the office worker who bought gyros for his team arrives. The smell from the gyros attracts Helen's glare. His co-workers wave him off, and he ducks into the breakroom.

Hess sniffs and yells, "Dammit! That vendor smells even stronger now! HELEN! Get the doorman and security on the phone, now!"

Coal Alliance Brain Trust

Genesis 9:5 "And for your lifeblood I will surely demand an accounting from each human being."

Earlier the same morning, Madison, heading up Climate League Action Network, known as CAN, plans to crash the CA board meeting. The team is in an abandoned warehouse on the East River. Gathered around a makeshift table, an old door on top of shipping crates, the team pours over the hand drawn schematic of the plans.

Nolan reviews the plans with the team "Initial entry is through the loading dock avoiding the front desk; then, Madison, Hannah and I will put on service worker overalls. enter through the storage rooms and up the service elevator. There are no cameras. If we back-in to the far end of the dock, the gate Guard can't see there."

Uly looks on, intermittently asking about what some of the symbols mean.

"This is a stairway." explains Nolan, "and these are air ducts for the air conditioning." Uly looks up from the plans and says he will take the air ducts to the 50th floor. Nolan protests, "But my plan is to use smoke bombs and flares in the air ducts. You won't be able to breath!"

Uly places his right hand on Nolan's shoulder, looks him the eye "No need for pyrotechnics. We do not want to flood the entire building with smoke and fear. Our focus is the 50th floor, the boardroom. The CEO and board members are the decision-makers. Leave the air ducts for me."

Madison asks, "When do the guards change their shift?" "It's interesting," Nolan perks up and continues, "They are hourly and there is no graveyard shift. Weird, but it is our chance to enter undetected."

Hannah interjects, "It's a cost-saving procedure. I guess they figure there's nothing worth stealing."

Uly raises his brow and wryly comments, "Nobody wants coal before it is a diamond." The team laughs.

Nolan nods his head slowly, "Good one!" Hannah and Madison share a look. They recognize a certain subservience Nolan has shown Uly over the past few weeks. Madison takes Hannah aside.

"What is with Nolan? Some kinda bromance with Uly?" Hannah chortles, "I'm not sure Nolan knows what romance is, actually" and in a mildly derisive tone, "Lord knows I've tried but I can't compete with good 'ol Mom."

Madison makes a face and adds, "Father figures aren't much better."

Both giggle a bit and return to the plan review.

Madison announces, "Sorry to break up the guy talk but we have a disruption to deliver. Our good friends at the Coal Alliance need our guidance."

Nolan offers, "I'll schedule an Uber ride. I have a coupon." Madison gently places her left hand on his shoulder, "No one goes to a disruption in an Uber. I borrowed a van early this morning."

Hannah quickly adds, "She means procured, via hotwire. The things you learn in prison."

Madison corrects Hannah's description, "Facility. Women's Detention Facility."

Nolan, protests, "but, but..."

Hannah urges Nolan, "Hurry up. Your plan better work, or we'll end up in a 'Facility'." Hannah finishes the sentence with the requisite air quotes.

It is just before dawn, as Uly requested. The morning traffic is tough and leaving early ensures they will be in the building before 8:30.

The CAN team arrives at the Coal Alliance building

The van, marked with Building Maintenance decals, backs up to the far end to loading dock. Nolan uses his lock decoder, opening the secured entrance to the service area.

Hannah hands out the coveralls as their disguise.

Madison sees Uly go a different direction. He enters a stairwell labeled MECHANICAL ROOM.

She shouts after him, "Uly wait! Your uniform!" He turns, puts a finger to his lips as a signal to be quiet; then motions for her to continue through the loading dock. Madison takes out her pack of Gitanes. It is empty. She tosses them toward the trash can, missing, like always.

Once in the basement area, Uly locates the main air ducts. He rises through them and up to the 50th floor where the Coal Alliance boardroom is headquartered. Dropping from a ceiling vent he is dressed in his trademark white suit, and a black cape with red silk lining.

Uly silently approaches the guard from behind and says, "I have a meeting with Renfield Hess. Please direct me to the boardroom."

The guard begins to answer but is startled to see him in full costume, "You're not a board member! How did you get on this floor?" Then, after a moment to gather himself, he says sternly, "You will need to clear security before..."

Uly raises his hand, and the Guard is frozen, only his eyes are moving. They reveal his fear as they widen. Uly calmly bends his head toward the Guard's neck. The Guard's eyes follow him as he is still frozen stiff. We see a slight wince from the guard's body, Uly pulls away, using a pocket square to wipe his lips. The Guard's eyes roll back in his head as Uly gently lowers him to the ground. A small pool of blood forms by the Guard's neck. Uly looks at the blood as the pool slowly grows and, in a whisper, says, "You will be fine, Rest now".

Uly meets the team at the service elevator. They walk down the marble floors and along the rare species of mahogany paneled walls. As the team turns down the hallway approaching the entrance to the board room, they see the Guard sprawled out on the floor.

Hannah asks, her voice quavering, "Is he dead?"

Uly says, "I don't kill. I preserve. He'll be fine in a couple hours. He just needs to gather himself."

Hannah looks over to Nolan, "I think he's dead".

Nolan looked at the Guard on the floor, "Naw, I can see he's breathing. He isn't dead. But Uly sure is weird". He looks up at Hannah and nods toward Uly, "What is with the cape?"

The CA meeting is underway. Peering through the glass doors they see Hess explaining their economic condition is dependent on a certain law not passing through the state legislature. During Hess's presentation, the board talk amongst each other, picking over the pastries and coffee on a platter in the center of the conference table.

Madison and Uly, Hannah and Nolan are hidden just outside where they can overhear Hess's presentation: "The essential message to the public, and more importantly, to our investors, is that we have not harmed the planet. We have helped humanity. We fueled the industrial revolution. The historical improvements we made possible in the workplace reduced injuries, increased wages and were the core of creating a middle class."

The board members are smiling, brushing crumbs from their coats, slurping coffee from CA mugs, and shaking their heads in agreement. The board members remain anonymous per CA corporate regulations. Each has seating placard with their designation BM1, BM2 and so forth.

BM1 in a most righteous tone pronounces, "The main reason for my service on this board is to see that the progress, the human benefits we make possible continues."

BM2 chuckles, "The generous stock options don't hurt, either!" They all laugh. Several reach for more pastries on a platter in the center of the conference table.

A buzzer sounds and the small red-light flashes. Hess seizes the remote and turns off the large screen monitor. Helen enters and places a small dish in front of Hess's chair at the head of the conference table. "Your Bavarian Cream, sir." Helen exits, closing the doors behind her. The red light ceases to flash.

Hess looks over his gluttonous board, "Well folks, it is not all rainbows and lollipops." The monitor is turned back on. "We have climate activists ready to stand in our way. Protests at our storage facilities. There are even increased attacks on our offshore testing projects in the Florida reef."

BM3 interjects "And they are using speed boats with gasoline engines. Stinking hypocrites."

Hess continues with a serious tone, "There are plans I have set underway. CA will put an end to these disruptive actions. The most threatening group is CAN.

BM3 leans forward in a hushed tone, "That's the CLIMATE ACTION NETWORK. Yeah. CAN."

Hess continues, "They have started using aggressive, even militaristic guerilla tactics. CA is engaging a force of ex-military veterans. They will meet these tactics with asymmetrical responses. It won't be pretty."

BM1 expresses concern, "Aren't we risking really bad press if we are sponsoring these countermeasures?"

Hess smiles and responds, "We have arm's length deniability. The security team has made sure CA is never associated with this effort."

Some board member's body language reveals their discomfort with the harsh plans Hess suggested.

BM1 interjects, "I sit on several energy boards. I cannot afford, nor can they, for any slip ups."

Hess commands their attention, "Listen. Therefore, you are *anonymous* board members. You are simply BMs. Your professional status is protected."

BM3 proudly states, "I am happy being a BM. No know needs to know my role here."

The Board Members begin to fully realize they are about to take actions making climate change reduction take much longer.

Perhaps make it impossible. The Board Members start to chatter among themselves.

BM3 turns to BM2, "I personally am not against efforts to preserve our planet."

BM2, bites into the remainder of her prune Danish. Still chewing she responds, "Me neither. But I don't want to end up in the poor house because of these terrorists."

BM1 chimes in, "We will need some fancy accounting to cover this expense. Any idea what the hit on next quarter's books will be?"

Hess wipes the corner of his mouth, clearing away the last of his Bavarian Cream, "The expense will not hit the books in any form. This is covert. I should not need to remind you none of this leaves this room."

BM3 looks up from his tablet, "Is there any way to use this as a tax deduction? I mean this operation could be beneficial on several levels."

Hess reacts with a snarl, "CA will have nothing to do with it. No paper trail will exist. Nobody is to speak of this, ever." Hess walks over to BM3 and bends down to his face, "Sometimes you are money grubbing idiot."

BM3 shrinks further into his chair with each syllable. "If your family didn't own the biggest coal processing plant in West Virginia you would still be managing the family company parties making sure everybody got their favorite donut. How you ever became a U.S. Senator I'll never know."

Madison whispers to Uly, "Now. We must go in now and take advantage of their doubts."

Nolan decodes the secure lock. Uly nods in agreement signals to the others to follow him and boldly walk into the boardroom. The buzzer sounds and the red-light flashes.

The door bursts open with Uly and the team walking in front of the presentation monitor. Uly is face-to-face with Hess. The board members are startled and shift in their seats, but none get up.

Hess does not flinch, and steps a bit closer to Uly, "Who the hell are you? How did you get in here?"

Uly smiles slightly, "We made our own appointment."

Hannah nudges Madison to speak up, "Go on, tell 'em why we're here, what we want from them".

Madison steps between Hess and Uly, looking at Hess and rapidly turning back and forth to the board members she announces, "We are CAN!" The board members respond in a collective gasp.

Madison continues, "We come in peace, for now. We will not let CA continue to harm our precious planet and our limited resources. We all need to live a decent life."

Madison feels a surge of confidence, "I grew up on a farm in rural Idaho. I know what having a working infrastructure means to having a good life. And that is the point! Preserving the world by reducing our contribution to global warming is the only path we have to help future generations and every species on earth".

While Hannah is speaking BM1 writes on a recycled notepad 'Do you think they have guns?' and carefully slides it to BM2.

Hess laughs at Madison, "You naive trollop, and your cosplay misfits- The noble Count, the computer geek, (and gesturing disdainfully to Hannah) and the token dyke. HA!"

Hess addresses the board, "This is what we are up against. Broadway wanna-be's, snail darter lovers, and basement dwellers, geeks still living with their trailer trash mothers."

Nolan screams, "You leave my mom out of this!"

Uly uses a hand to gently restrain Nolan, nudging him back to the group.

The board members are chuckling and there is cacophonous crosstalk.

Hess continues, "This ragtag group is what challenges us?"

BM3, "Oh Hess, your plans are overkill for these sorry souls."

The laughing continues.

Madison's pleasant demeanor turns visibly angry and shouts, "Do not underestimate our resolve! I know what sacrifice is. I have slit the throat of animals to feed my family. My family survived. Will yours?"

Hannah and Nolan look at each other. Nolan bursts out, "Where the hell did that come from? We're not murderers!"

Hannah adds matter-of-factly, "Except maybe for the Guard."

BM3 says to the board members, "We need more security here."

Hess has had enough of this theatre and decides to threaten the CAN team, "I am calling security. They will have the police take care of you, and if you continue to annoy us, I will personally see that you are finished as disruptors of progress, as disruptors of anything."

Uly steps up to Hess and gently waves his hand, and Hess is frozen, and like the Guard, only his eyes are showing expression.

The board members' chatter turns to yells. "Guard, Guard!" "Does he have a gun?" "Is there a bomb?"

 BM3 jumps up to run to the door. Uly waves his hand, this time with anger, and the board member is frozen in stride. One board member starts to hyperventilate, another is crying while trying to call out on his cell phone.

Uly waves once more and all are frozen.

Uly sternly states, "We have no more patience with you."

Hannah and Nolan are freaked out. "My God, what did he do to them?"

Nolan responds. "It's mass hypnosis. I read about it. I guess it works".

Madison asks Uly if they can hear her. He nods affirming they can.

Madison speaks up, "We came here to reason with you. And you still won't listen. The planet is at risk. All we are asking for, all that needs to be done, is to find ways to progress while doing less harm to our planet. Climate change is real. Human contribution to it is real. We need to do our part. We need you to do your part. It may cost you some profits in the near term. But you must consider the lives, the quality of life for those generations that follow."

Uly turns to Madison, "I have a solution." He snaps his fingers and the board members' heads fall back and their eyes roll up into their heads, mouths open.

Uly intones this command, "You will announce that CA is beginning a program to reduce pollution, reduce carbon emissions from coal processing, and from the coal and petroleum products you manufacture. You will work for three years at half your annual pay, suspend all your bonuses, and not exercise any of your stock options."

Hess's eyes are showing extreme stress and anger. Uly snaps his finger and the board members' eyes roll back and mouths close.

Uly turns to Hess and whispers in his ear, "Hess, you will do the right thing. You will not interfere. You will exit as CEO of the CA. You will no longer be heard from in any way or by any means. You are done. You will do the right thing."

Madison looks worried about the tone of Uly's commands and asks "Uly, what are you saying? How do you know any of this will happen?" Uly looks at Madison, touches her chin, "This is what I do."

Hannah and Nolan both say, "But the police, we'll be arrested."

Uly calmly states, "No one will call security. The police will not arrest our team." He gestures gently to the board members, "They will not remember we were even here."

Madison asks, "And Hess"?

Uly pauses, looks at Madison, "Let's roll".

Aftermath

Romans 12:21 "Do not be overcome by evil but overcome evil with good."

After driving all night, the CAN team huddles in their makeshift offices just outside the Everglades. Hannah and Nolan return with provisions for a meal. The hibachi is glowing, and hamburgers are cooking.

"Rare, please." Uly requests, "Very rare."

Nolan looks up from the grill, "I usually like them well done, but I'll try rare this time. Sounds interesting."

Hannah scoffs, "Sounds bloody gruesome to me. Make mine charcoal."

Madison has been sitting in the corner. Brooding over the actions of the day before, she expresses her doubts.

Madison takes out her pack of cigarettes. One left. She crumples tosses the wrapper on the table.

Uly flicks it with a finger so to read the labels, "Gitanes. I did not know that people in the USA would smoke such a cigarette."

Madison ignores his slight, "The issue is morality. Is it moral to make people, against their will, do what you want? How is this different than slavery? Or outright oppression?"

Madison begins pacing, back and, arguing with herself as much as with the team. She draws deeply on her smoke. "That is not what we want. CAN seeks to convince people of the moral imperative regarding climate. Future generations, if they are to survive, need a planet that is livable. It is so basic. Are we reduced to hypnotizing the movers and shakers into making the right decision? Is that even tenable in the long run?"

Uly uses a small piece of the paper shopping bag to wipe a bit of the blood from the hamburger from the corner of his mouth. "You presume these people follow the same moral compass. They do not. Their allegiance is to whoever pays them. There is no moral imperative, only a profit imperative. As a business, the defined goal is to create wealth."

Uly now stands, gesturing with a clear plastic cup filled with an inexpensive cabernet. "It is a fool's errand trying to change the tenets of commerce. They are pre-history. Business is the basis of human interaction. In this regard, my goals for saving humanity align with any businessperson."

The team is following Uly as he walks the room. "We need humans to survive, to do business with, to create life. If you cannot make it clear that business will benefit from reducing the human impact on climate change, you have no purpose worth their time."

Madison, emotional, responds in a strained voice, "For fuck sake, we ARE the humans. That is in fact what we are trying to do. My objection, our objection to what happened in the CA boardroom is about your tactics. The security guard, bleeding on the floor. The board members frozen, commanded to do your bidding. Finally, the CEO, Mr. Hess. You hypnotized him, mesmerized his soul. He jumped out a window from the 50th floor! Bloody guards and suicides are reprehensible and cannot be part of our methods."

Uly calmly but coldly responds, "You are needlessly, even foolishly naïve. You worry about a guard who lost some blood and is now fully recovered. You fret over a deeply bitter and troubled CEO. These souls I know. That is the power I bring. This is the advantage you have with me on the team. Yes, the weak will fall."

Uly approaches Madison and looks straight into her eyes, "But the strong and the good will survive and bring forth future generations. And nobody's hands are clean in making this so."

Angered, Madison retorts, "You sound like you want a super race. We are not about anything like that. This is horrible. You are heartless."

Uly furtively responds, "Oh, I have a heart. I have a will to live. And you, Madison, so conflicted, so blinded by your own righteousness. I know you have supported the Pro-Choice movement. Is that not a death wish on the unwanted? Those children no one can afford to raise properly. A super race of the well-heeled is your choice. Children of parents that can afford to raise a child. And talk about greed? The woman who becomes pregnant and chooses an abortion because she has a career to tend to?"

Madison is raging, "These are apples and oranges issues. One has nothing to do with the other."

Uly adopts a superior tone, almost singing the words "Ah, but they do. You are making moral choices. You are willing to force them on others. It was you that wanted to break into the boardroom. It was you who asked for my help. You didn't qualify what tactics were acceptable, or as you put it, moral. Own your role here. Completely. No one is innocent, everyone is guilty. We all have a stake in the outcome. The only question? Is it worth the cost?"

"You, right now, are unable to make that decision." Uly continues, "You are a politician in this battle for survival. Arm's length from the fog of war, from the inevitable terrors. If you cannot stomach what is needed to be done, do not question my motives. There is no difference in your vision of survival and mine. That is what drew us together. We are not different; we both want to survive."

Hannah is seething in silence. In a burst of emotion, she attacks Uly, "I've heard enough of your superior logic. It's not ok to leave a person on the floor in a pool of blood. I don't care what you say. Enough of your moral equivalencies. You're evil. You use evil powers. Who the hell are you? What the hell are you?"

Uly has never been challenged like this. For his twenty centuries of life, being a vampire was enough. He never had to answer for who he is, for what he is.

Uly displays his anger for the first time. It is a new feeling, one that defies his cool self-control, "Who are you to question me? I don't kill. That does make me better. And as for who I am…well I am the means you all have chosen to partner with to meet your goals. And you think you are better than me? You are not! My needs define who I am. How I meet those needs is justification itself."

Nolan speaks up for the first time. "And there you have it! The ends justify the means. He's right. We are evil. We are guilty."

Madison yells, "Stop! Everyone stop. We do have a goal. We do have a moral compass. I don't accept your characterization of climate change as forcing my moral standards. Climate change is everyone's goal, or at least should be. No one. No one wants to perish because it was too expensive to do the right thing. That's giving up hope. Eat, drink and be merry is not a solution. It is not the answer."

Madison chokes up, "Damn it, I won't cry." Gathers herself, "This is my life mission. I know it's vital. To me. To the world. I just can't… I can't be the one who resorts to violence. I tried and it was wrong."

A silence takes hold. Uly looks around engaging the eyes of each team member. He speaks in a measured tone, "Think of me what you will. I have a past. A long and complicated legacy. I will not discuss it. I will not force my ways onto you."

Uly has their attention and stokes their passion. "But we have something in common. Something important and vital. We must find a way to work together. Take direct action. Forceful, non-lethal, undeterred. I do not kill."

Madison, voice shaky, responds, "The power of the mission is to save us all, to save humanity. That is what motivates all of us. We must be a team. We must work together. And no one can die from our actions. Everyone?"

They all put their hands out, forming a circle.

Uly looks at everyone, "I know the term. This is very Kum-By-Yah."

Amused, Nolan asks, "Kum-By-Yah? You are so Millennial."

Uly responds, "That's Multi-Millennial to you."

Uly and Nolan laugh, the others groan.

Return to the Office

Micah 7:8 "Though I have fallen, I will rise."

Walking down the hallway of the Immigration and Customs Enforcement Eastern Annex offices, the strobing fluorescents remind him of his waning career, close to burning out and becoming toxic, useless waste. He reaches for the doorknob. Nick hesitates.

He hates this office. This building. This new assignment. He is a reject from the elite Airborne Object Identification (AOI) unit. Nick's dogged pursuit of sightings of unidentified aliens, the non-humankind, got him labeled as crazy cop, an agent out of control. With a lengthy career and near retirement, the government assigned him to ICE. To investigate aliens.

The human relations team did not seem to know the difference between Mexicans looking to work and space beings trying to invade the earth.

Nick turns the doorknob. Again, for the umpteenth time, the loose handle cuts the top of his index finger, right on the knuckle. "Shit. That's gonna hurt for a week." Blood appears slowly. Nick stopped taking the baby aspirin his doctor prescribed. Now cuts, even small ones, flow the blood slowly. Nick prefers it that way.

Eddie looks up from his desk. Mouth full, with crumbs from the prune Danish fall on his shirt. He raises his coffee cup as a salute to Nick's arrival. Nick nods his recognition. Reaching his desk, Nick sees a note attached to his desk lamp "See me!" signed ASB. This is his boss, Abe Bostick.

Nick sighs and lays this thread bare backpack across his desk. Jimmy Burroughs' sits face to face with Nick. He rarely shares his thoughts or his case findings. Uncharacteristically he chooses to look up and engage Nick, "Abe's pissed. Pissed at you." Nick does not respond. Jimmy continues with "Straw that broke his back he claims."

Nick still does not react and continues putting his coat on the rack next to their joined desks.

"Nick!" The call comes from the dark end of the office. Abe is sticking his head out, disembodied by the inadequate lighting. He withdraws into his office like a turtle into his shell. He leaves the door open.

Nick sighs again and walks the aisle to Abe's office.

Abe continues, his voice becoming shrill. "You took the car for the entire day. We had two skiffs of Haitians come onshore and the team had to take an Uber! The South Florida media had a field day."

-ICE agents use Uber to capture poor refugees-

"What a headline."

Abe goes on with his rant while Nick daydreams recalling his days with the AOI force. Each agent had their own car, a Hummer for fuck's sake.

Abe raises his voice, "Nick! Are you listening?"

Nick nods. He removes the car keys from his shirt pocket and places them on Abe's desk. He rises from the chair and starts out the door.

Abe, yelling at this point shouts, "I'm not done with you!"

Nick continues down the aisle and out the door into the hallway. He pushes the door to the restroom too hard; it bangs against the wall. The last stall, like Superman, is Nick's fortress of solitude. He latches the door, drops his trousers, lowers the horseshoe toilet seat, and claims his asylum. Head buried in his hands; he hears the door open. The footsteps echo and stop at his stall. Nick sees Abe's wingtips through the space under the stall door.

"Not only the car but you take my stall as well. Piece of work, Nick. You are a piece of work."

Incident Call

Isaiah 5:20 "Woe to those who call evil good and good evil"

Pulling up to the Coal Alliance office building, Nick and Eddie double park the agency minivan. Police cars and emergency vehicles with lights flashing are randomly parked on the street and the sidewalk.

Nick struggles opening the damaged door. "You have to reach out and open it with the door handle." Eddie advises Nick. The door opens and bangs the ambulance next to them.

Eddie stays inside, finishing off a chocolate cruller with a coffee chaser.

Nick is immediately confronted by NYPD uniform. "This area's restricted."

Nick pulls out his badge, displaying it in the officer's face.

The officer waves it away. "What the fuck is ICE?"

A voice from behind the officer calls out "I called them. Let 'em through."

"Detective Pinscher." Dick Pinscher introduces himself and reaches to shake hands. "We saw your BOLO. I want to show you something."

Nick shoulders his way past the officer.

"I'm with him," Eddie turns sideways and catches up with Nick. "What prompted the call? What did you see?" Nick asks.

Pinscher continues, "We have an image. The dude matches the BOLO description. There is something weird though."

"Yeah?" Nick looks at the iPad.

"Look at this video. The CCTV was hacked, wasn't working. But the Guard's bodycam was running."

Nick peering at the screen, "I just see the hallway."

Pinscher tells him to keep looking. "Guard's glasses fell over his bodycam."

At that moment, the image of Uly appears in the video.

Pinscher excitedly, "See? We can only see him after the glasses cover the bodycam."

Uly is pulling away from the Guard's face and wipes a bit of blood from the corner of his mouth.

"Forensics tells me the glasses are polarizing lenses, which made him visible to the camera." Pinscher looks at Nick, "I know your background. You're the supernatural expert. What kind of weird human is this guy?"

Nick looks up, "Preternatural. Maybe human. Have a copy sent to me."

Nick hands Pinscher his card. "So where is the jumper?"

"He was sent to the medical examiner. Along with the vendor cart. They have the equipment to extract Hess's body."

Eddie quickly, "When can we speak to the Guard?"

"He's upstairs." Pinscher motions with his head. "They'll move him once the Medi-vac helicopter is here. He was pure white when I saw him, but still breathing." Nick begins to turn, Pinscher continues, "We also found this on the loading dock." Pinscher holds up an evidence bag. "A rare brand to be found here, in the states. I know them from when I was stationed in Marseilles. Gitanes. No person in their right mind would smoke them." Nick looks over the bag. Nick adds, "And nobody here seems to smoke them. Could be a lead."

The sound of the helicopter is heard getting louder as it passes over the skyscrapers. Police quickly cordon off the street. Nick and Eddie look at each other.

Nick heads back to the minivan. Eddie tells detective Pinscher they will catch up with the guard at the hospital as he follows Nick. Pinscher hands Eddie his card, "Call me if you find something."

Eddie nods, looking at the card he says, "Dick Pinscher. That had to tough growing up." Pinscher has already walked back to cordoned area.

Eddie climbs in the driver seat and places the card in the sun visor. He turns to Nick. "Why did you leave? You know

Pinscher is gonna make you jump through hoops to get to the guard."

Nick, looking forward, eyes fixed on something distant. "Pinscher will keep a lid on everything. This is his beat."

Nick reaches in his coat and pulls out a piece of paper. "One of the uniforms slipped me this." He hands the note to Eddie. Out loud, Eddie reads "I was the first one to the guard. He was semi-conscious, babbling about an invisible man. I saw two marks on his neck dripping blood."

Looking up at Nick asks, "Was it the red-head? She gave you this?"

Nick pauses and nods in confirmation.

"What does it mean?" Eddie asks, scratching his head.

Nick explains, "It means if word gets out an invisible blood sucker is on the loose the public will panic. It's best the NYPD takes the heat for keeping this quiet. It also helps us. No publicity means the perp won't know we're on to him."

Nick takes back the note, "But all Abe is gonna say is that we found an eyewitness to an invisible man."

Eddie shoots a quick look at Nick and shakes his head in agreement. Nick, still looking at the note, and rubs it between his thumb and forefinger. He thinks out loud, "18 pt. matte weave, embellished with gold foil for the badge. They have a budget." "Let's get to the morgue. We need to see if Hess has all his corpuscles."

Eddie turns the key, but the engine fails to start. He tries again and the engine rumbles, then backfires loudly causing all the cops to drop to the ground, their guns pointing at the minivan.

Nick gives a simple beauty queen wave as they drive off, backfiring the whole time.

Morgue, Maglis, and Rigor Mortis

Matthew 26:52 "…for all who draw the sword will die by the sword."

The fluorescent lights strobed. The hallway was sterile white tile, a subway tunnel to a certain purgatory. The morgue reminded him of his office.

Eddie is gasping, "The stink!"

"Mercaptans and formaldehyde," Nick grumbled, "the nectars of embalming."

Eddie blurts out, "I think I am gonna barf. Where's the bathroom?"

Nick pushed through the double doors. There, in the middle of the room, the vendor cart with Hess planted in the middle. Only his legs are visible. Nick looks over the evidence. Reaching up with a pen, he eyes the shoes.

"Humph, Bruno Maglis. Only the best for Hess."

Nick is interrupted by the medical examiner, "You can look, but don't touch, I'm M.E. Dinmont. What was it you needed to see, besides his shoes?

"Well, Miss…"

Dinmont interrupts, "You can call me Dani."

Nick caught the wink. But romance in a morgue was not his thing. "I'm looking to see any wounds. Wounds before he hit the griddle."

"I see you're with ICE. Seems odd you'd be doing business in a morgue. Guess there's a first time for everything."

Eddie, back from the restroom, looks over to Nick. "All I know is I ain't eatin' hot dogs from street vendors any time soon."

The body is hoisted out of the cart and dropped onto the exam table. Rigor mortis kept Hess's body in the ready position ballplayers use just as the ball leaves the pitcher's hand.

"Jackie, straighten out the corpse." The morgue assistant pulls the limbs into a resting state allowing Hess to lay flat.

Eddie bellies up to the exam table. He leans in to have a closer look at the neck. "Any tooth marks?" Suddenly Hess's eyes pop open. Eddie jumps back, slips, and falls into the body chambers. Grabbing a handle to keep from falling, the door opens, and a body slides out on the tray just enough to see the head with a screwdriver in it.

Eddie screams, "I'm gonna barf." And runs back out to the restroom.

Dani chuckles, "I'm guessing it's your friend's first experience with taphonomic convulsion?"

Nick is looking at the screwdriver.

Dani nods her head, "Yeah, the screwdriver. They claim it was an accident." Jackie slides the body back and closes the chamber door.

Nick explains to Dani, "I need to see if there are any punctures into veins. Neck, wrists, anywhere they are exposed. They're evidence."

"The whole damn body is evidence, ICE-man." Dani checks and looks back at Nick.

"Don't see any entry wounds. What is it you're after?"

"Please send the report on how much blood is in his body."

"You'll get it tomorrow. You still haven't told me what you're looking for."

"Vampires."

Dani guffaws. "Ha! Just go to the bank holding my mortgage. They'll suck the life out of anything right down to the last corpuscle. Vampires, what next."

Nick nods his thanks to Dani and turns to exit the morgue.

Dani has Hess's head in her hands twisting it from side to side. "Jackie, get me the cordless bone saw. This cranium is thick. Make sure it has a fresh battery."

Oil and Water

Ezekial 4:16 "Look! I am about to disrupt the source."

The curtain separating the sleeping area in the CAN headquarters is moved aside. A dim light spreads across the beds.

"Hannah. Hannah. Wake up."

Groggy, Hannah mumbles, "What? You had your nightmare again?"

Madison excitedly answers, "No, no. I just got a lead that the Oil Initiative League is planning an event in the Lake Worth Lagoon. It promotes their off-shore oil drilling program."

Hannah, somewhat confused, "Don't you ever sleep? So, what are we going to do? When is it?"

"The press conference is at 10 a.m. tomorrow, at low tide. We need SCUBA gear and a couple divers. That's you and Nolan." Hannah lies back down with the pillow over her head.

"Wake up! We have no time to waste." Madison pulls off the pillow and throws it toward Nolan's bed.

"What? Huh? What's going on?" Nolan squints from the light coming through the entry.

Madison raises her voice. "C'mon. Let's go."

Uly is at the van, dressed in a nautical captain's jacket and cap. "Hurry along. We must finish before dawn, so we are not discovered."

Nolan and Hannah look at Uly, then each other. They say in unison, "Fashionista." And the team drives off.

A few minutes later their van pulls up to Davy Jones Dive Shop. Madison turns to Nolan, "Are you sure he'll show up?"

Nolan looks out the window across the parking lot. "Yeah. He's a good guy. Even at 3:00 a.m., he'll show. There he is now."

Hannah is shocked, "He's in a wheelchair! A motorized wheelchair."

Nolan exits the car and turns back to say, "You stay in here, I'll deal with Howie." Nolan pauses a moment, turns back and says through the open window, "Howie was an underwater welder. He worked on oil rigs, yeah, the Deep-Sea Horizon. They sent him down in the middle of it all. When it blew they pulled him up too fast. He didn't decompress. Yeah, he supports us, what we're trying to do."

Nolan comes back in few minutes loaded with tanks and wetsuits. "I also got the shark attractant."

Hannah says, "You mean repellant."

Madison interrupts, "No. Attractant. We want every shark within a mile surrounding the barge they will be on in the middle of the lagoon. We hang chum from the edges of the barge and the sharks and everything else will going crazy. Plus, we have red dye."

Madison turns to Nolan, "Did you get the dye?"

Nolan smiles, "Right here. Blood red, and eco-safe! 30 vials. There will be blood!"

Madison details the plan. They will approach the barge before dawn. Chum the barge and set the trigger mechanism on the red dye vials. "Imagine the visuals. The TV cameras will have a field day. Sharks jumping on the barge, the red water churning. People freaking out."

Madison is giddy with excitement. "I have the press release ready, from us, CAN, claiming responsibility. With the OPEC reps on the barge, we're sure to make the international news."

Uly reminds the team that time is short, "We must get started. We've only a few hours remaining."

As the eastern sky begins to lighten, Hannah and Nolan emerge from the water. The gear is stowed in the van. The team takes a moment to reflect.

Hannah asks Uly, "So are you going to hypnotize the entire barge, or will they be too busy trying not to get bitten?"

Uly answers, "They will understand the message. We will be a safe distance from the event."

Uly turns to Madison, "You are a brilliant tactician. I have known many throughout time. You are a special and talented leader."

Hannah and Nolan agree with "Wow" and "You go girl" praise.

Madison is the last to get in the van. She pauses and looks back over the bay as the dawn takes hold. "We are a team. We are good."

CAN headquarters meeting room

Later that morning the team turns on the small TV in the office. Nolan and Madison are eager to see if their actions made the news. A banner showing "BREAKING NEWS" in bold letters in a chyron message *OIL and OPEC pranked with sharks and red dye*.

Nolan reaches over the TV and cranks up the volume.

Announcer: "Trey Norton here with breaking news. Just moments ago, at a news event in Lake Worth Lagoon put on by the Oil Institute League and OPEC was left in chaos. Sharks began attacking the barge in the lagoon where the event was just starting.

"Blood red water surrounded the barge and frenzied sharks flew out of the water landing at people's feet. One camera operator was slightly injured and taken to the local emergency room. Others were treated by EMTs at the scene.

"The governor has promised quick action by the state police and the FBI has been called in. Our reporter Tiffany Valderama is on the scene. Tiffany?"

"Trey, the scene here is chaotic but thankfully no serious injuries are reported at this time. I have with me police commander…"

Tiffany is interrupted by Trey who is holding the earpiece in his ear. "Sorry for interrupting Tiffany, this just in. An activist group calling themselves CAN, CLIMATE ACTION NETWORK is claiming responsibility for the attack on the OIL-OPEC press event.

"We have photos provided by the FBI. The first is Madison Bathory, a known felon, who is believed to be the leader of the terrorist group. The other photo is a person of interest. This is the only known picture showing his face. If you have any information on this person, call 202-555-4321. Again, 202-555-4321. We will have more after a word from our sponsors."

The team looks at each other. Hannah yells, "We made the news! We're famous!"

Madison looking at each member of the team, points her finger and intones, "It worked. Now we have their attention. Now they know we mean business. Now we can make a difference."

Uly stands and turns to the group gathered around the TV, "Fame. It is not our friend."

Madison looks at Uly, "Why aren't you happy? You are part, a big part of our success."

Uly looks straight into Madison's eyes, "I was part of a team. An equal part. And no more or less responsible for the success of these invasive disruptions. Madison, you are the leader. The achievement is from your leadership and vision."

Nolan and Hannah are absorbed in surfing every TV station and every website that is reporting on the incident.

Uly and Madison step into the downstairs rooms. "Uly, you and your abilities made this possible We all shared the vision, the goal to bring climate change to the forefront."

Uly smiles, it is the first time Madison has seen him smile. Uly starts to speak. Madison places her finger on his lips. She rises on her toes and kisses him. Madison pulls back. Looks over Uly's face. Uly pulls her close and they passionately kiss. Excited, Madison whispers, "Let's get out of here. The Westin Hotel isn't far from here."

Uly looks deep into Madison's eyes, "I have no money, no identification."

Madison smiles, "I have everything we need. Everything you need."

Early the next morning in the hotel

Madison and Uly lay in bed at the Westin Hotel. Both stare at the ceiling. Moments pass in silence. Madison turns to Uly, whispering "I never thought I could love. I mean, there is no one who made me feel this way. Powerful. Righteous."

Uly doesn't move, only a slight sigh. "We have turned a corner. You and I. Love is complex. Complicating."

Madison doesn't like what she is hearing, "Something's wrong. You're troubled. Am I wrong about us? About love?"

Uly turns to her, "No Madison. You are not wrong. You are in love."

"What do you mean? I don't understand."

"I cannot love. I cannot be loved. It is my curse."

"Wow, you're feeling vulnerable. I don't want to hurt you. I won't hurt you. If I am moving too fast, too aggressively…"

"Stop. It is my fate. And I do not want that fate to be yours as well."

Madison is confused. "Oh, Uly. Is there someone else? Are you married?"

"In my entire life there has been no one. I never knew my mother. Only an archangel watched over me to ensure the curse was never lifted from my brow."

Madison, "I have no idea what you are talking about. Are you religious? Have I offended your beliefs? Tell me what is going on?"

Uly implores Madison, "Just come with me. I'll explain what I can. Tonight. We won't need the car. Just come."

Uly gets out of the bed, "I must go now. I will see you at sunset."

Madison falls back into the pillow, "Why is my life so weird?"

A Cemetery is No Place to Rest

Ezekiel 37:12 "Behold, O My people, I will open your graves and cause you to come up from your graves"

Grethe Skogman is busy gathering the last of her archive, packing it carefully in banker boxes. These papers must be removed from the sinking building Grethe has occupied for the past 13 years. These papers, the years of research are her legacy.

The small radio sitting on the edge of the work desk blares out a news announcement, "OIL-OPEC event disrupted by terrorists. The FBI is reporting the leader of CAN, the Climate Action Network is now wanted on charges related terrorist activities. Madison Bathory was last seen in New York City after a terrorist break-in at the Coal Alliance building in Manhattan. At least one death was reported. Bathory is believed to be in south Florida, possibly armed. If you have any…"

Grethe switches off the radio. "Madison!" Grethe breathes through her teeth, "I knew she would resurface."

Grethe opens her workstation browser to go to the online news service 'Florida Now'. The report on the attack is the lead story. There are pictures of the barge, the red sea water and sharks nipping at the people.

Grethe chuckles as she scrolls down to picture of Madison, "Ah Maddy, your youth has left you. The rigors of prison and the underground world you live in is taking its toll."

Scrolling down further, Grethe gasps, "Uly! The bastard has returned."

ICE office, Eastern Division Annex

It's late in the day. The trail for the mystery man and his partner in crime, Madison Bathory is getting cold. No leads, no tips, nothing from the FBI or Interpol.

Nick makes his way down the hall to the office, jacket over his arm, fluorescent lights flickering. Holding a Dutch Bros large coffee with no cream, in one hand, he carefully touches only the outer edge of the door handle, avoiding the sharp metal edge. Nick does not want another week of dollar store bandages falling off into his lunch.

Just then Eddie bursts through the door knocking the coffee cup out of Nick's hand. The no-spill cap does its job and only a few drops escape from the sippy hole in the top.

"Oh, sorry 'bout that, Nick. Coffee is ok though." Eddie retrieves the coffee, handing it to Nick. "You can use some of my bandages for that cut. Top drawer, right side. They're Anti-bacterial. I get 'em at the dollar store."

Nick holds the coffee in the bloody hand, keeping the door from closing with his foot.

"You got a call. A tip on that Bathory character and her mystery boyfriend. Some professor knows who the guy is. Wouldn't tell me, said you know her. Skogman (Skawg-man)"

Nick corrects Eddie, "Skow-man. The 'G' is silent."

Eddie hurries down the hall and turns to announce he is going for donuts. "Whaddaya want?"

Nick doesn't hesitate. "Bavarian cream."

Professor Grethe Skogman tells Nick they need to meet. "Why waste valuable time? Just give his name and the FBI will get everything on him."

Grethe insists on meeting, "The FBI will not have anything on him. He is totally unknown. He only exists in the shadows."

"Yeah, I saw the bodycam video. He only shows up through sunglass lenses."

"There is much more, Agent Charles. Be at the Gator Tail Cafe at six this evening."

"I have other cases to deal with…"

"This will be your only chance to learn who he is. You want your immigrant? Be there."

With that ultimatum, the line goes dead.

"Hello? Hello? Shit, she's crazy." Nick taps his finger on the top of the coffee cup, it has gone cold. He has not had a sip yet.

The Gator Tail Cafe

It's ten past six and Grethe has not shown. Nick sips the last of his Dutch Bros large coffee.

"Sir, we aren't supposed to allow outside drinks. Are you going to order?"

Looking just behind the server, Nick sees Grethe. "Professor, over here." He waves his hand.

"See your date finally arrived. Lucky you. Coffee for both of you?"

Grethe dryly says, "We won't be staying." The server throws up her hands, and leaves muttering mild curses.

"Where are we going?"

"Follow me Agent Charles."

Grethe walks at a hurried pace down the street and into an alley leading to encroaching waters of the swamp only a few hundred yards from the main part of town. Nick is eyeing the eight-foot-long spear Grethe is carrying.

"What's with the long spear. Are we expecting savages to attack?"

"Alligators," Grethe answers dryly, "They charge lightning fast, but only for six feet. This gives me a chance to drive it drive down their throat."

"Humph. I'm trusting my 9mm SIG."

Grethe chuckles, "Better aim well. Have to hit them between the eyes. Gators can lunge more than once."

A ground fog is hugging the edges of the water. It's difficult to know where the shoreline is. The undergrowth is thick, the brush rises to their shoulders.

"How much further? I don't like this...I don't like it at all." Nick brushes the blood-sucking mosquitos from his face.

"Over there, Agent Charles. Just beyond the cattails." Grethe points with her walking stick.

"Looks like a graveyard. Is it an old church?"

"No church for this cemetery. No graves either. All tombs. All above ground. With the water level rising they'll soon be gone. And, Agent Charles, that is why we are here."

"I'm losing patience, and interest. First your stories are hard to believe. Now you're not telling any stories. Spill the beans or I am outta here."

Grethe says nothing, Nick turns to leave.

"Wait!" Grethe exclaims. "We need to enter the grounds."

Nick swats another mosquito, "Got him." A small blood stain surrounds the crushed insect, "Damn, she got me."

The ground fog has overwhelmed them, now becoming a swirling grey veil with each step they take towards the cemetery. Only the tops of the tombs are visible above the fog. The red mangroves mask the sky, the branches dripping dew, the roots skeletal fingers grabbing at their feet.

Grethe and Nick enter the through the rusty wrought iron gate. The wrenching sound of the gate opening scares the Mangrove Cuckoos, their screeching cackle announcing the human invaders. Nick ducks down as birds dive at his head.

Grethe yells, "There it is! That is what we came for."

The fog has moved away from one tomb. It is shaped like a casket. It has thirteen inverted crucifixes adorning the top. Above towers, the stele with another inverted crucifix. This one has the Christ figure upside down.

The ledger is covered in overgrown weeds. Nick struggles with the thick vines. Tiny blossoms release a scent of death; thorns puncture his skin leaving bloody streaks on his hands. A chiseled engraving is visible, *Aici zace Clementine. Fie ca ea să se ridice din nou.*

Loyalty vs. Love

1 Peter 3:4 "I will see you again and your heart will rejoice."

Uly and Madison meet just after sunset near the edge of town. The fog has risen and slowly swallows each building into its grey mist. There is no moon this night. It is cold for a Florida night. Madison wears a sweater and a coat, Uly has his cape.

Uly sees that Madison is hesitating, "It's safe to walk through this part."

"The ground is too wet. I need my boots." Madison explains.

Uly calmly says, "You won't need them. Let me carry you."

"The path is old and uneven. I…" Uly sweeps Madison into his arms.

"Oh Uly." Madison puts her arms around his neck, and they continue down the path.

Grethe brushes the last of the vines from the ledger. She mumbles something.

Nick, unable to understand what she said, "Say that again. What language is it?"

"It's Cyrillic. An old version from centuries ago."

Nick scoffs, "You speak ancient serial? Circulus? Whatever?"

"Of course," Grethe muses, "Here lays Clementina. May she rise again."

"And that means…?", Nick asks impatiently.

"It means we are in the right place. I believe at the right time."

Nick, growing leery addresses Grethe. "Professor, no offense, but you haven't told me anything. Nothing but BS mysteries. I don't need any more mosquito bites. I'm outta here. Don't call me with any more tips, wild goose chases, or non-existent human life forms. No time to be taken for a ride. I'm done."

Just as Nick turns to leave, the birds start the loud cackle and burst in a chaotic flight circling the tomb.

"Holy shit!" Nick covers his head from the swooping birds. And just as suddenly, they stop. The silence has an eerie hum, almost a buzz. The mosquitos have disappeared, no sound of crickets or bullfrogs.

Grethe puts her finger to her lips warning Nick to stay silent. A dim light appears from behind the tomb. It grows brighter.

Out of the swirling mist Uly, with Madison in his arms, lands at the foot of the tomb.

Grethe announces the couple's entrance with a sneer, "Agent Charles, meet your illegal immigrant. You have no idea how illegal he is. And dear Madison, you have taken up with the wrong person. A blood-sucking liar. He will steal your soul along with a pint or two."

Nick turns to Grethe, "You know them! And you withheld this from me? I'm putting you all under arrest."

Nick pulls his gun. "Hands behind your backs. Turn around." No one moves.

Madison confronts Nick, "So you're going to shoot all of us?"

Uly moves toward Nick, "Put your gun away. We mean no harm."

Grethe cries out, "Bullshit, you blood sucking mutant."

Nick warns Uly, "Not a step closer."

Nick pulls back the hammer. Uly stops in his tracks, and slowly waves his hand. Nick is frozen, just like the security guard and CA board members. Eyes twitching back and forth, Nick's face is frozen in terror.

Grethe screams, "You're mine now mutant!" She charges Uly with the gator pole. Madison yells, "Uly look out!"

Uly warns Grethe, "I'll never be a specimen in one of your jars!" With one hand, Uly swiftly swats the spear spiking it in the ground. Grethe's momentum pole vaults her up and over Uly. She lands face up on the top of the tomb, impaled by the inverted crosses.

Grethe curses Uly. Madison is speechless, gasping for air. Uly walks over to Grethe, bends over to her face. "You will be OK.

Agent Charles' backup will be here soon. They will call for help."

"You bastard. You ruined my career when you lied to me. You promised to help me prove that mutant forms existed. And you never showed. You left me standing alone, ridiculed by my peers. I lost my position. I lost my funding. I lost my institute. You will keep building your army of followers who are enslaved by your evil powers. I will follow you to the ends of the earth. You won't get away with this. I swear on your mother's grave!"

Uly coolly responds. "You are on my mother's grave, Grethe. Enjoy it while it lasts."

Madison grabs Uly by the arm, "You can't just leave her here."

"I assure you; she will not die. Suffer? Yes. As have I. We must go. It is time for the team to go undercover and lay low."

Madison looks over at Nick, still frozen, sweat running down his face, "And for the agent?"

Uly walks over to Nick. He gently moves Nick's arm down, taking the gun and replacing it in the holster.

Madison asks, "Will he forget everything? Like the Board Members at CA?"

"No, Maddy. Agent Charles will remember every detail. But no one will believe him. He too must suffer, much like Grethe. They know too much but do nothing to make it better. That is what makes you, us, the team better for the world's future."

Madison is entranced, "Oh Uly. We have so much to do."

"Right now, we must leave." Uly again sweeps Madison into his arms, and they glide away into the night mist.

The backup for Nick finally arrives

"Hello! Nick where are you." Nick hears Eddie's voice but cannot respond.

"I see them. By the tomb." Several voices are heard as the backup team has arrived.

Eddie comes up to Nick, "Nick? NICK!" He waves his hand in front of Nick's face.

The EMT says, "He's in shock." Looking over at the tomb he sees Grethe, moaning and cursing. "Oh my god, what happened here?"

Eddie turns back to Nick, "Are you ok, buddy?"

The EMTs take Nick by his arms and throw a silver foil blanket over him. "We have to get him to the hospital."
Eddie asks about the Grethe, "What about her?"

The EMT looks him in the eye, "That will take some work."

Nick is placed in the back of the ambulance. He is incoherent, making no sense to anyone.

Captain Abe Bostick pulls up in an Uber. "Eddie, fill me in. Is Nick hurt?"

Eddie takes Abe several feet away from the ambulance. He was in shock. When he started coming to, he just babbled about floating people and mutant blood suckers."

"Vampires? Nick is gone off the deep end."

Eddie looks back at Nick, "Yeah, the deep end."

Abe pauses, "I'll have a Baker hold set for him. It'll be ready by the time the ambulance gets him there. Go with him. Make sure they give him something to take that frozen look off his face. It's creeping me out."

"You got it, Boss. Hey guys wait up." Eddie climbs the back of the ambulance.

Moving On

Galatians 6:9-10 "Let us not become weary in doing good."

"So, he's just leaving us, the team?" Nolan asks Madison.

Hannah adds, "Uly can't just go. We need his skills."

Madison tries to contain the growing fear, "Calm down. This was never a forever deal. Uly helped when and where he could. He never asked anything of us."

Hannah quips, "As long as we never asked him anything about his past."

Nolan joins in, "Yeah. Big blocker there. Who the hell is he anyway?"

Madison pulls out her pack of Gitanes, "Two left. The liquor store is out of these. Damn it."

Uly reaches in his jacket pocket, and hands a new pack to Madison. She just looks at him, eyes tearing.

Nolan flatly states, "You're bailing on us."

Hannah crumbles up the empty bag of chips she was eating and throws it the computer, "We're screwed without you Uly. You know that."

Uly confronts the team, "Madison, stop crying. Nolan, Hannah, stop putting yourselves down. Don't underestimate the powers you have. You all did the work. You all took the risks. And you all are still here. I expect you to continue your good works. Your mission to make the world aware of the danger climate change represents."

Uly looks each of the team in eye, "I have my mission too. It is not for you to know. It is mine and mine alone. I must go. The team will survive, the team will succeed. Humans will be better because of what you have done, and what you will do. Tonight, I must board the ship, under the cover of darkness. It requires your best effort and is your last mission with me. I need your help."

Uly looks at everyone and asks, "Are you with me? Can you help me as I have helped you?"

Hannah and Nolan look at each other. Madison, tears running down her face looks at Uly.

Nolan speaks first. "I am with you." He stands.

Hannah stands, "Me too."

Madison jumps into Uly's arms, "Me too. I am with you."

Nolan, a bit hesitant, "I had the container taken to the cargo docks. Everything, all the furniture you had is in there, including that extra coffin. Say why did you need…"

Madison interrupts, "Thanks Nolan. Thanks."

Uly smiles. It is the first time Nolan and Hannah have seen him smile.

 Nolan whimpers a bit, choking back tears.

Hannah turns abruptly, and says, head buried in her hands, "I'll miss you Uly."

Madison looks at Uly and then back at the team. "Four a.m. We'll take the van and our things. Just the basics. We're moving on from here. Four a.m."

The Morning Tides

Psalm 8:8 "Whatsoever passeth through the paths of the sea."

Eddie nods to the night nurse and enters Nick's hospital room. He gently touches Nick's shoulders. "Hey buddy. The hold is over. Doc says you're good to go."

Nick is groggy, but aware enough to realize he can check out of the mental ward. His incoherent stories about what happened in the cemetery, and his history of crazy encounters with extremely odd people, well his boss insisted he get help. Nick wasn't sure the number of drugs they put in his IV helped, but he knows he is getting out now.

Nick quickly gets dressed. Barely tucking in his dress shirt and letting his tie hang loose, he realizes these are the same clothes he checked in with three days ago. Even looking like a slob, he only wants to leave.

Getting into the car Nick confronts Eddie, "Who put me in there? Who committed me on a Baker hold?"

Eddie doesn't hesitate, "Abe ordered it." He quickly adds, "And I think he was right. For your own good. The doctors said you were way out there, buddy. Two days of babbling. The EMT gave you Midazolam. Not sure what else they gave once you were committed. I came by but you were totally zonked out. I mean dead to the world."

Nick nods, "Dead is what I feel like now. What happened to Professor Skogman?"

Eddie laughs, "A damn miracle. All those upside-down crucifixes missed her vital organs. Just flesh wounds. They released her yesterday. She lawyered up and won't say a word about what happened. Not sure about a connection with the tomb, though. There was nothing in the crypt."

Nick keeps going, "And what about this Uly character and Bathory the terrorist?"

Eddie pauses, takes a slight nervous look over to Nick. "Well Nick, Bathory …well there's no trace of her or the van they stole. Actually, no evidence she was at the scene except for a crumpled pack of some French cigarettes."

There is silence between the two.

Eddie starts to suggest a reason for Nick's condition, "The sight of the Professor impaled, that would shock the hell out of anybody."

Nick snaps back, "That wasn't it. That guy, the illegal immigrant did something to me. Maybe a dust, or some hypnotic trick. Shit I don't know. I still feel weird from the drugs."

The police radio in the car crackles, "Incident sighting at cargo docks. Possible ID on terrorist Madison Bathory and two others. Approach with caution. Do not proceed without backup."

Nick, "Let's go."

Eddie, "It's four in the morning, Nick. You need to go home. Nick, NOW!"

Mantee Bay container loading facility

Madison, Nolan, and Hannah stand on the dock. The *Carpathian Princess* blows its horn as it leaves the dock. The three team members stand and watch for several minutes as the ship grows smaller until its lights disappear.

Madison, "Did you get everything out of headquarters?"

Nolan, "Yeah we're good to go."

Hannah adds, "I left a couple clues. Total misdirects. Maps all marked up showing spots in North Carolina and West Virginia. They'll take the bait."

Madison agrees, "Yeah. They'll never look for us in Hollywood. The producer said he will interview us for his documentary, keep our faces in silhouette. By the time it's released we'll be long gone."

Madison pulls out the last of her Gitanes. She lights the cigarette with her last match, striking it with her thumb, convict style. The empty wrapper is tossed to the overflowing trash can but falls to the dock.

Nolan shouts, "Let's roll." The engine turns over, exhaust spews from the tailpipe, and with a couple backfires, they are off.

Later that morning, just before dawn

By the time Nick and Eddie arrive the place is crawling with ICE agents, local sheriffs, and the FBI. Eddie pulls in behind the CSI processing unit. Nick gets out and walks to the end of the dock. He just stares at the ocean. "I wonder where they go next. It could be anywhere." Nick pauses a moment. He faces Eddie, "I swear to you, the guy floated in the air. With Bathory in his arms. They could be anywhere."

Eddie just looks at Nick, shaking his head, "Nick, you need to stop telling that story." Nick just stares straight ahead, "Eddie, I fear that is just one part of the story."

Dawn breaks, the mosquitos rise from the swampy waters, Nick swats at them. He slaps one on his arm. The crushed insect is surrounded by a ring of Nick's blood. "Damn she got me. She got me."

Nick sees something on the dock. It is a crumpled cigarette wrapper, Gitanes. He slowly unfolds it. The Gypsy on the label smiles, winks her eye, and begins to slowly dance. Nick whispers, "Are you Clementina?"

Eddie walks over, "What is it, Nick?"

He looks up, "Nothing." He puts the wrapper in the trash bin, making sure it's buried deep inside.

Abe Bostick joins them on the dock. "Nick, you need to rest. We'll handle it from here."

Nick turns one more time, facing Abe and Eddie, "I swear..."

Eddie pats Nick on the shoulder, "It's the everglades Nick. Forget it."

A hollow shell of himself, Nick squints at the sun just over the horizon. "Yeah, the everglades."

About the Author

Robert Godwin is an award-winning screenwriter/filmmaker. Growing up in Burbank, California next door to Hollywood, it was inevitable he would be drawn to the stories on cinema screens. As a young teenager, fascinated by the power of visual imagery, he wrote his first stories.

In the cinema program at Los Angeles City College, and Art Center College of Design, he made his first film. A few decades later, Robert tapped into his film school experiences for the screenplay Hollywood Adjacent.

Together with his degrees in cinema and studio art, Robert holds an MBA in Marketing, all combining to fuel his vision of the sometimes uneasy relationship between art and business. During the between years, Robert pursued an unconventional career path, from teaching, photography, and movie marketing, all of which led him back to creative storytelling.